THAT'S FACTS-INATING!

THE WORLD OF SPORTS

Kidsbooks®

Kidsbooks®

Copyright © 2016, 2019 Kidsbooks, LLC
3535 West Peterson Avenue
Chicago, IL 60659

Every effort has been made to ensure all information in this book is correct.

Printed in China
101901032GD

Visit us at **www.kidsbookspublishing.com**

DO YOU KNOW...

TUG OF WAR WAS ONCE AN **OLYMPIC EVENT?**

Skiing was a form of **transportation** before it was **a sport?**

THE FIRST BASEBALL HATS WERE MADE OF STRAW?

Get ready to learn **tons** of other **fascinating facts** in this **fun-filled book** about **sports!**

Kite-flying is a professional sport in Thailand.

Olympic gold medals are made mostly of silver.

THE FASTEST SPEED

ever recorded on a bicycle was

152.2 MPH

by Olympic Cyclist John Howard in 1985.

THREE CONSECUTIVE **STRIKES** IN BOWLING IS CALLED A TURKEY.

ALL MAJOR LEAGUE UMPIRES ARE REQUIRED TO WEAR BLACK UNDERWEAR ON THE JOB, IN THE EVENT THAT THEIR PANTS RIP.

A basketball is exactly HALF THE DIAMETER of a basketball hoop.

Ice hockey players believe they will win a game if they tap the goalie on his shin pads before a game.

BOXING BECAME A LEGAL SPORT IN ENGLAND IN 1901.

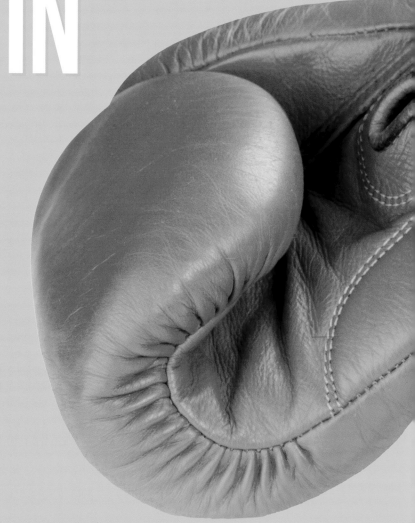

A tennis match takes about **2.5** hours.

ROWING

is the oldest COLLEGE SPORT in America.

The most **COMMON SCORE** in a soccer **WORLD CUP FINALS** match is **1-0.**

Skateboarding came about in the 1950s when surfers in California wanted to try surfing on pavement.

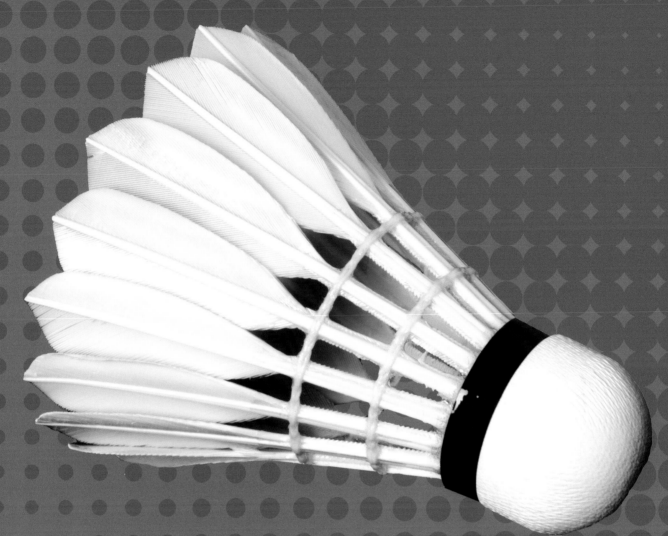

BADMINTON

was created by **British military** stationed in **British India** in the **1800s.**

TUG OF WAR
EVENT FROM

WAS AN OLYMPIC 1900 TO 1920.

ROLLER SKATES were first used for a theatrical STAGE PERFORMANCE in LONDON in 1743.

THE NATIONAL SPORT OF NEW ZEALAND IS RUGBY.

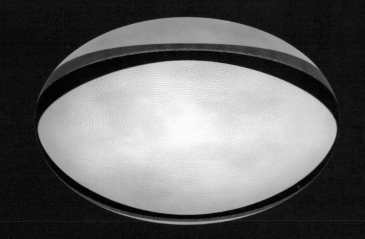

THE SHORTEST BADMINTON MATCH ONLY LASTED FOR 6 MINUTES.

BASKETBALL became an official OLYMPIC EVENT at the SUMMER GAMES in BERLIN, GERMANY, in 1936.

BOSTON CELTICS WORLD CHAMPIONS

BOSTON CELTICS 1959 WORLD CHAMPIONS

BOSTON CELTICS 1960 WORLD CHAMPIONS

BOSTON CELTICS 1964 WORLD CHAMPIONS

BOSTON CELTICS 1965 WORLD CHAMPIONS

BOSTON CELTICS 1966 WORLD CHAMPIONS

BO C

BOSTON CELTICS 1976 WORLD CHAMPIONS

BOSTON CELTICS 1981 WORLD CHAMPIONS

BOSTON CELTICS 1984 WORLD CHAMPIONS

BOSTON CELTICS 1986 WORLD CHAMPIONS

BOSTON CELTICS 2008 WORLD CHAMPIONS

CH

23
2

THE BOSTON CELTICS HAVE WON THE MOST NBA CHAMPIONSHIPS (17).

The longest recorded putt made in golf is

375
feet.

THE COLOR YELLOW WAS ADDED TO TENNIS BALLS IN 1972 TO MAKE THEM MORE VISIBLE TO TELEVISION VIEWERS.

When thrown by a Major League pitcher, the average baseball

ROTATES

15 TIMES

before being hit by the bat.

When a pole-vaulter lands, he may absorb up to 20,000 pounds of pressure per square inch on the joints of his thighbones.

The term **KARATE** is a combination of two words:

KARA (empty) and **TE** (hand).

The longest tennis match on record was played in 2010 at Wimbledon between John Isner and Nicolas Mahut. It lasted 11 hours and 5 minutes, played over 3 days.

THE Baltimore Ravens ARE NOT NAMED AFTER the bird, BUT ACTUALLY FOR the poem "The Raven" BY Edgar Allan Poe, A BALTIMORE RESIDENT.

There are
318,979,564,000
ways

of playing the first four turns in a game of chess.

Skiing

was a form of **transportation** dating back to prehistoric times before it became a sport.

The United States has won a total of 2,520 medals at the Summer Olympic Games, more than any other country.

The national sport of Brazil is capoeira—a martial art that combines elements of dance, acrobatics, and music.

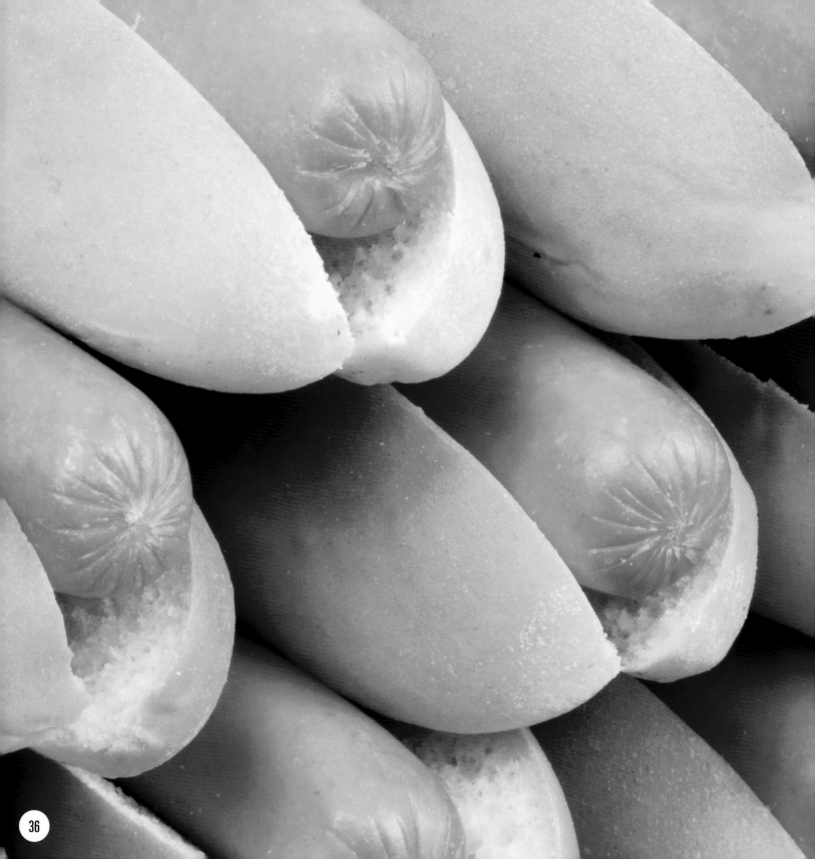

12,000
pounds of
hot dogs
are sold
during a
single race
weekend
at
NASCAR's
Talladega
track.

Japan is home to the world's largest bowling alley— The Inazawa Grand Bowl, which has 116 lanes.

About **54,250** tennis balls are used during the **WIMBLEDON CHAMPIONSHIPS,** equivalent to the **WEIGHT** of the average **HIPPO.**

The fastest knockout in Pro Boxing history happened in 10.5 seconds.

The football circular huddle was invented in 1892 by a deaf quarterback, who wanted to hide his hand signals from opposing players.

The three-point shot in basketball was introduced in the late 1960s by the American Basketball Association.

In baseball, a "can of corn" refers to a fly ball that is easy to catch.

THE JEWELRY COMPANY TIFFANY & CO. MAKES THE U.S. OPEN TENNIS CHAMPIONSHIP TROPHY.

UNTIL RECENTLY, ICE SKATERS WERE ONLY ALLOWED TO SKATE TO INSTRUMENTAL MUSIC. NEW RULES NOW ALLOW SKATERS TO USE VOCAL MUSIC WITH LYRICS IN THEIR PROGRAMS.

THE ANCIENT GREEKS
AWARDED
VICTORY CROWNS
MADE OF
OLIVE
BRANCHES
TO
WINNERS
OF THE ORIGINAL
OLYMPIC
GAMES.

FREESTYLE MOTOCROSS produces some of the worst **WIPEOUTS** in the history of action sports—from **RUPTURED SPLEENS** and **FRACTURED COLLARBONES** to **SHATTERED ANKLES.**

BRAZIL IS THE ONLY NATION TO HAVE

PARTICIPATED IN EVERY WORLD CUP FINALS TOURNAMENT.

SUPER BOWL SUNDAY IS THE **SECOND LARGEST** DAY OF FOOD **CONSUMPTION** IN THE **UNITED STATES,** AFTER **THANKSGIVING.'**

There are about 34,000

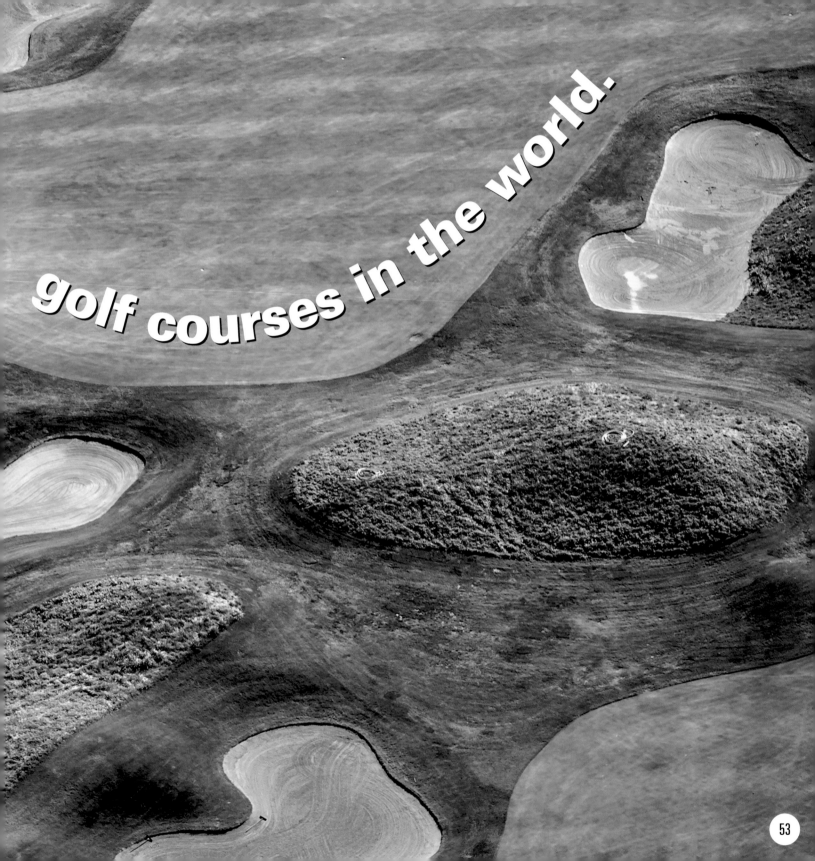

golf courses in the world.

The average life span of a Major League baseball is 6 to 7 pitches.

THE NATIONAL BASEBALL HALL OF FAME AND MUSEUM IS LOCATED IN COOPERSTOWN, NEW YORK, AND SERVES AS THE CENTRAL POINT FOR THE STUDY OF THE HISTORY OF BASEBALL IN THE UNITED STATES.

IN THE 1994 WORLD CUP, ALL 11 PLAYERS ON BULGARIA'S TEAM HAD LAST NAMES THAT ENDED WITH THE LETTERS "OV."

NBA POINT GUARDS ARE USUALLY THE SHORTEST PLAYERS ON THE TEAM, EVEN THOUGH THEIR

AVERAGE HEIGHT IS 6'3".

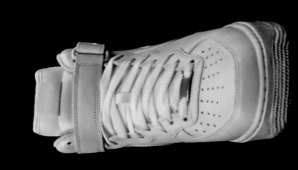

VOLLEYBALL, originally called **MINTONETTE,** was invented by **William G. Morgan** in 1895 as a **LESS INTENSE** team sport than basketball. As YMCA director in Holyoke, Massachusetts, Morgan found volleyball more **SUITABLE** for **OLDER** members of the club.

In rowing, the most difficult and most important seat in the boat is called the stroke.

The person in this seat is responsible for setting the tempo and speed of strokes.

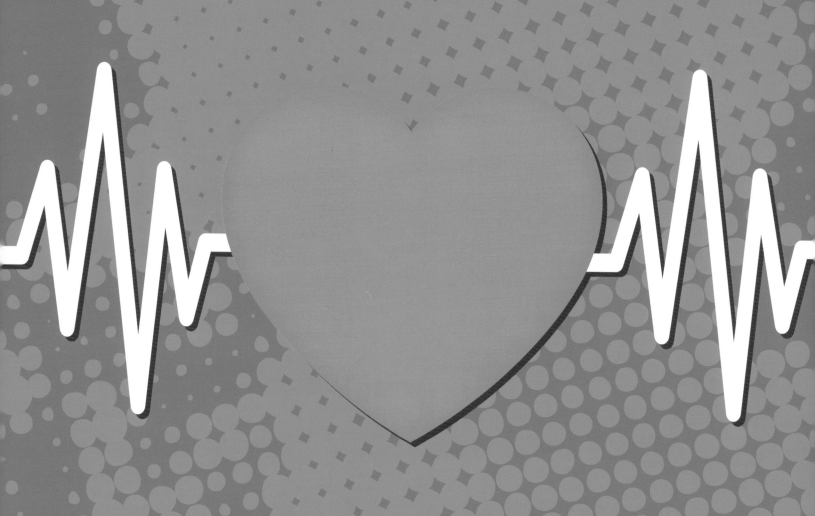

THE AVERAGE MARATHON RUNNER'S HEART BEATS ABOUT 160 TIMES PER MINUTE DURING A RACE. AN AVERAGE ADULT'S HEART BEATS ABOUT 60 TO 100 TIMES A MINUTE AT REST.

The OLYMPIC FLAG, five rings—BLUE, BLACK, RED, YELLOW, GREEN—on a WHITE background, was designed to represent every COLOR used in the FLAGS of participating NATIONS.

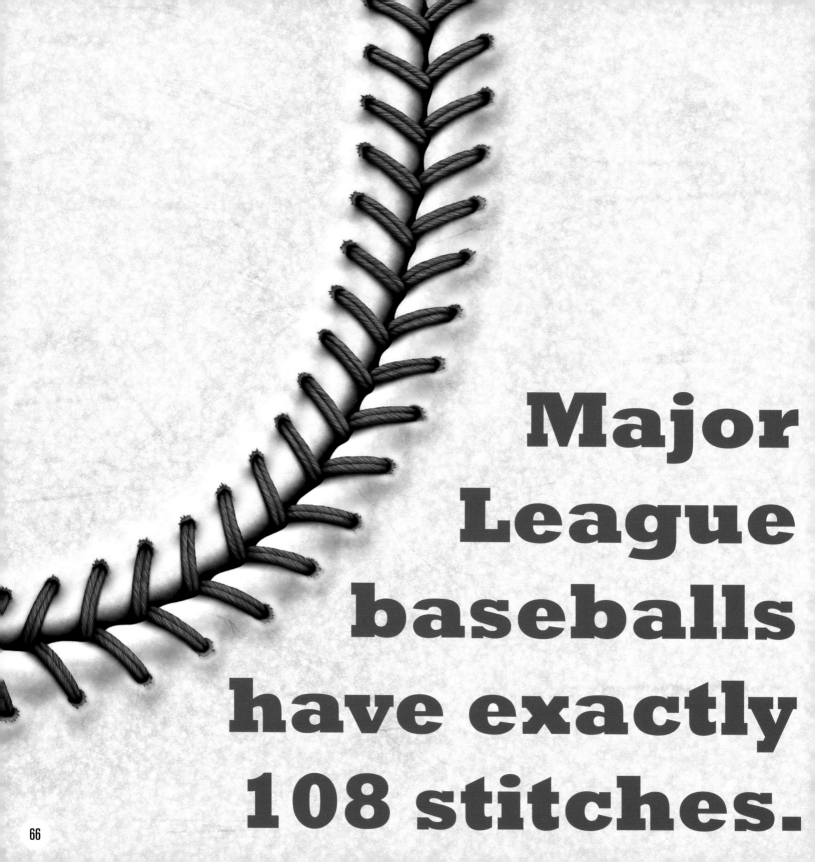

Major League baseballs have exactly 108 stitches.

THE BLADE OF A MODERN SPEED SKATE IS LONGER AND THINNER THAN THAT OF A HOCKEY OR FIGURE SKATE.

The first basketball hoops were actually just peach baskets, and the first backboards were made of wire mesh.

THE TERM "HOME RUN" WAS ORIGINALLY USED IN CRICKET, NOT BASEBALL.

In 1964, *JUDO* was the first MARTIAL ART to be accepted as an OLYMPIC SPORT.

CABER TOSS

is a traditional **SCOTTISH** sport in which competitors toss a large **WOODEN** pole called a **CABER,** which is usually almost 20 **FEET TALL** and weighs **175 POUNDS.**

HOCKEY PUCKS ARE FROZEN BEFORE EACH GAME SO THAT THEY DO NOT BOUNCE DURING THE GAME.

THE FIRST MODERN OLYMPIC GAMES WERE HELD IN ATHENS, GREECE, IN 1896.

The oldest female gymnast at the 2012 Summer Olympics was 37 years old.

THE STANLEY CUP WAS ORIGINALLY ONLY SEVEN INCHES HIGH AND IS NOW MORE THAN 35 INCHES HIGH.

PITTSBURGH,

Pennsylvania, is the only city that has the **SAME** **TEAM COLORS** for all its **MAJOR LEAGUE** sports teams— **BLACK** and **GOLD.**

The national sport of **ENGLAND** is **CRICKET.**

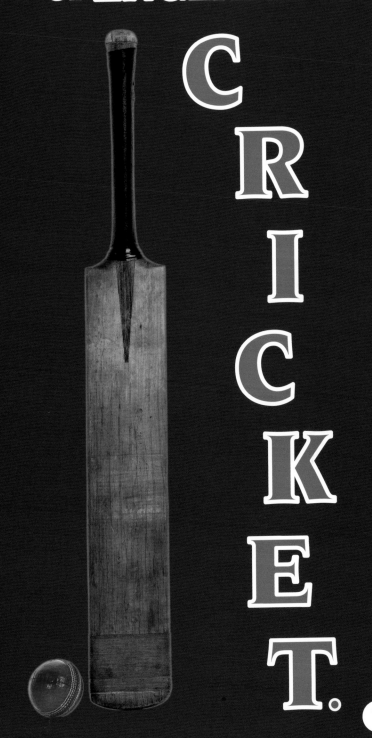

FOOTBALL (called SOCCER in the United States) is the most-attended sport in the world.

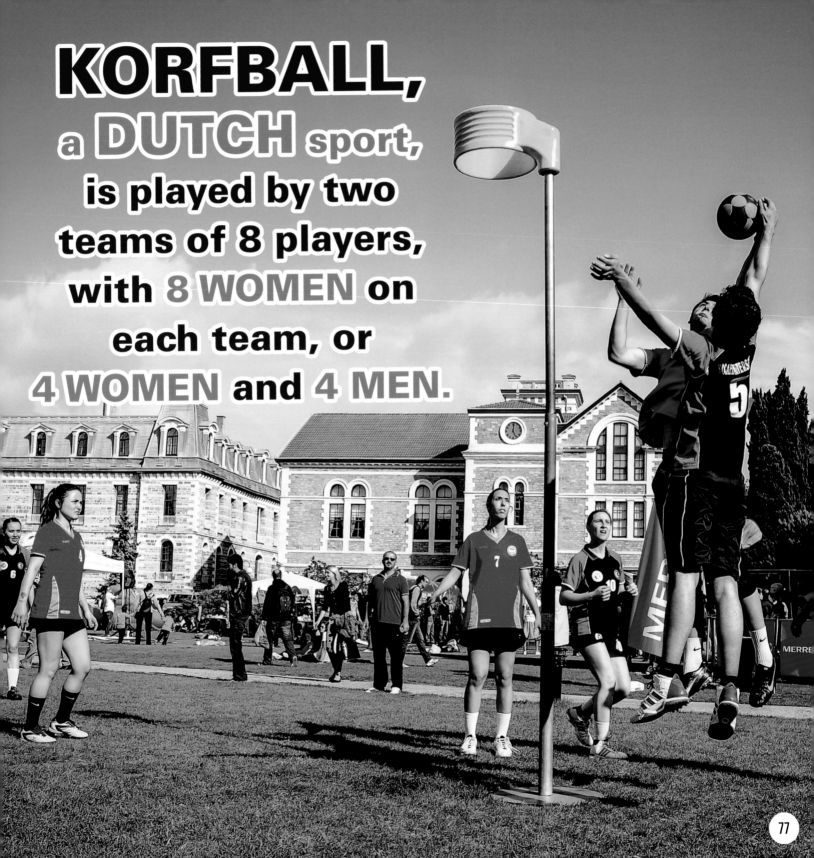

KORFBALL, a **DUTCH** sport, is played by two teams of 8 players, with 8 **WOMEN** on each team, or 4 **WOMEN** and 4 **MEN.**

The tennis term "love" is derived from l'oeuf, the French word for "egg," symbolizing zero.

TENNIS

was originally played with

BARE HANDS.

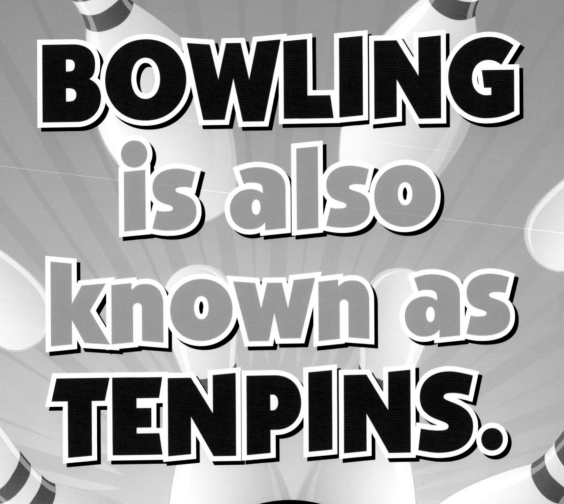

BOWLING is also known as TENPINS.

Astronaut ALAN SHEPARD smuggled a GOLF BALL and CLUB onto the APOLLO 14 mission and then played GOLF on the moon.

THE FIRST BASEBALL HATS WERE MADE OF STRAW.

Lacrosse is of **NATIVE AMERICAN** origin.

Many NASCAR nitrogen instead of air.

drivers use

in their tires

The **KENTUCKY DERBY** is the **OLDEST** continually held sporting event in the **UNITED STATES.** It has been held since **1875.**

SNOWBOARDING

became an **Olympic** sport in **1998.**

It takes about **3,000 COWS** to supply the **NATIONAL FOOTBALL LEAGUE** with enough **LEATHER** for a year's supply of **FOOTBALLS.**

There has **NEVER** been a **DOCUMENTED** perfect bracket for MARCH MADNESS.

1ST ROUND	2ND ROUND	REG SEMIS	REG FINALS	NAT SEMIS	CHAMPIONSHIP	NAT SEMIS	REG FINALS	REG SEMIS	2ND ROUND	1ST ROUND

EAST

MIDWEST

SOUTH

WEST

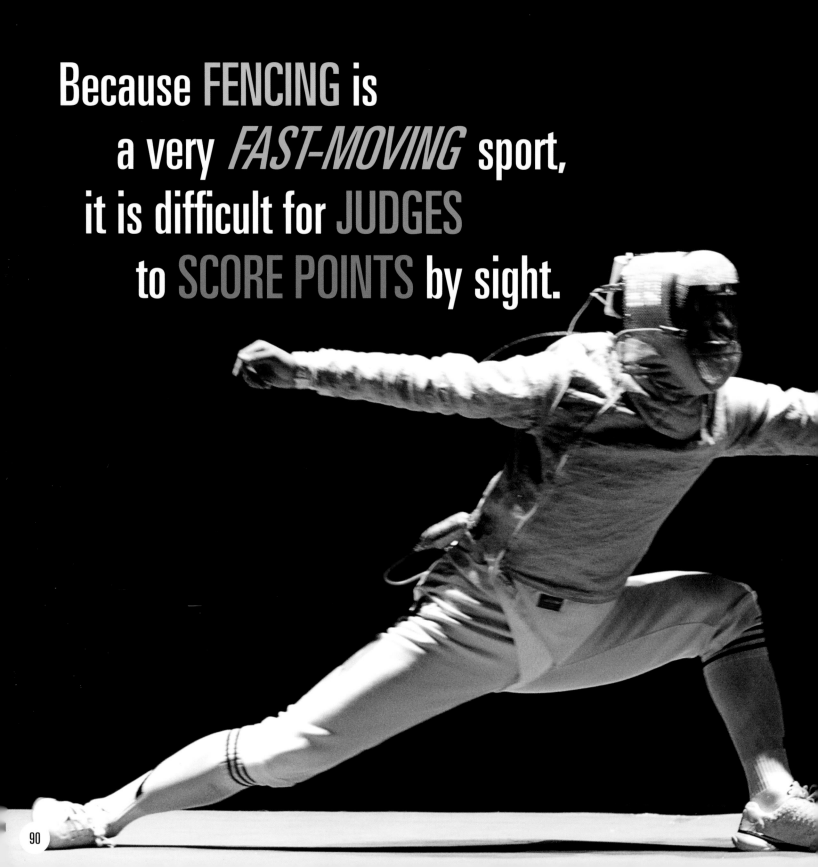

Because FENCING is a very *FAST-MOVING* sport, it is difficult for JUDGES to SCORE POINTS by sight.

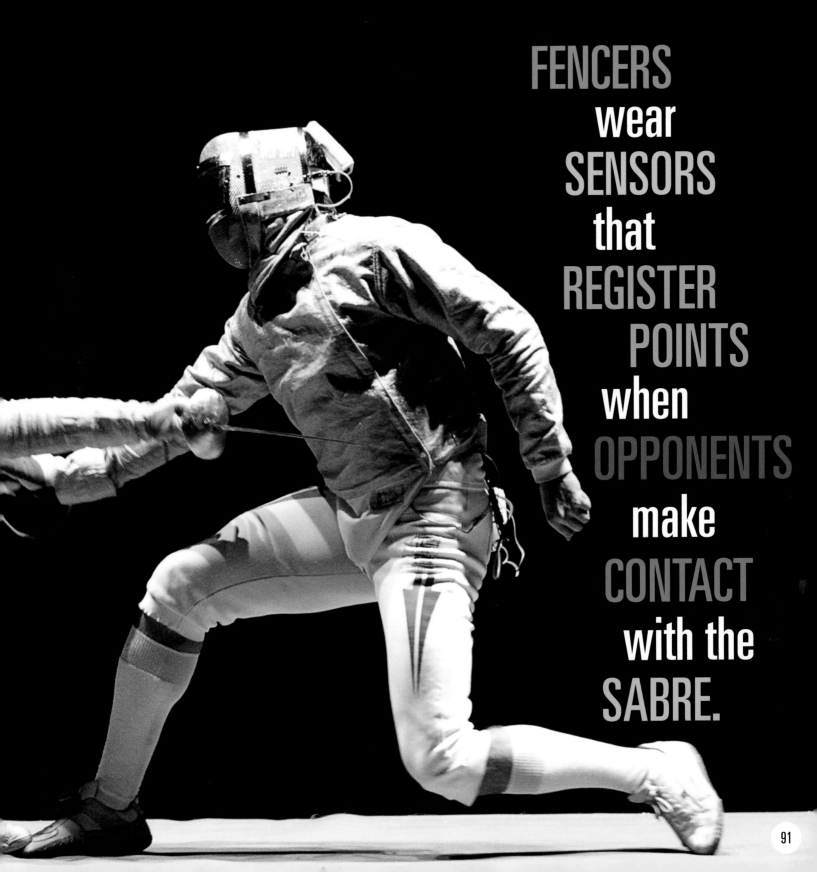

FENCERS wear SENSORS that REGISTER POINTS when OPPONENTS make CONTACT with the SABRE.

Common baseball SUPERSTITIONS include TAPPING the BAT on the PLATE, purposely STEPPING ON or AVOIDING STEPPING ON the FOUL LINE when taking the field, and NOT TALKING about a NO-HITTER or PERFECT GAME while a game is in progress.

The OLDEST tennis court was built in 1530 for KING Henry VIII OF England.

In the OLYMPICS, only WOMEN COMPETE IN BALANCE BEAM.

The official DISTANCE of a MARATHON is 26.2 MILES.

THE FIRST WIMBLEDON TOURNAMENT WAS HELD IN 1877.

The NATIONAL SPORT
of RUSSIA is
BANDY,
which is similar to ICE HOCKEY.

More people are struck by LIGHTNING when FISHING than any other leisure activity.

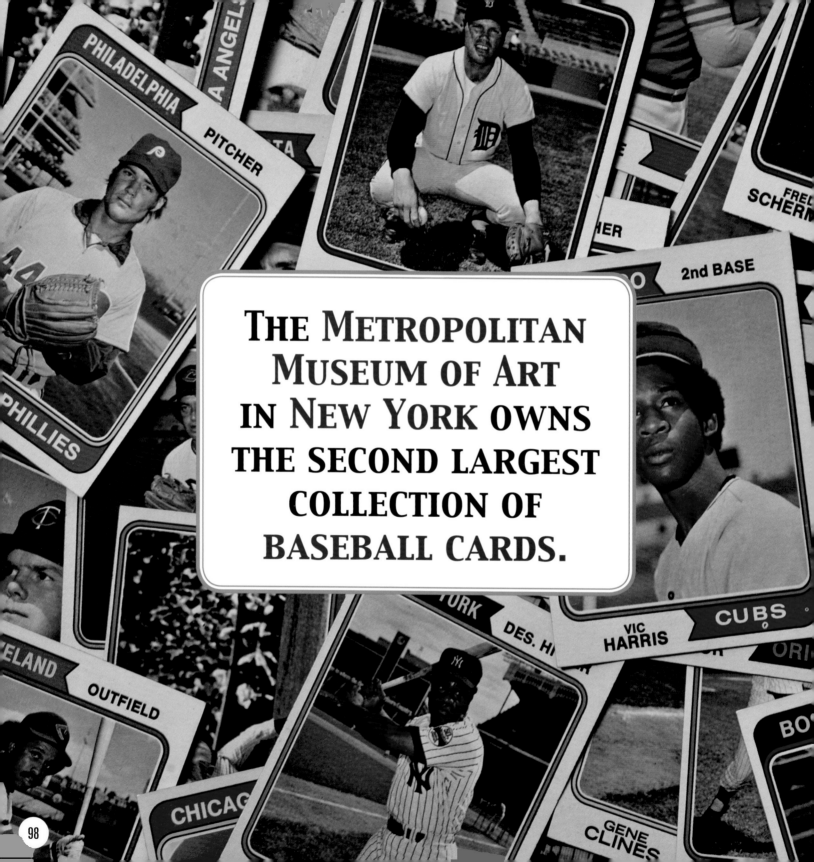

THE METROPOLITAN MUSEUM OF ART IN NEW YORK OWNS THE SECOND LARGEST COLLECTION OF BASEBALL CARDS.

Judo and karate students are awarded colored belts to indicate their ability in the sport. In both sports, a level 1 student, or 1st kyu, wears a brown belt.

The WORKOUT in SWIMMING comes from moving AGAINST the FORCE, or RESISTANCE, of the WATER,

which is **EQUAL** to more than **TEN TIMES** the **FORCE** of **AIR.**

GERMANY'S national **FOOTBALL** (soccer) team was **BANNED** from participating in the **WORLD CUP** of 1950 in Brazil as **PUNISHMENT** for its aggression in **WORLD WAR II.**

GYMNASTS use CHALK to IMPROVE their grip, ABSORB sweat, and KEEP their hands DRY.

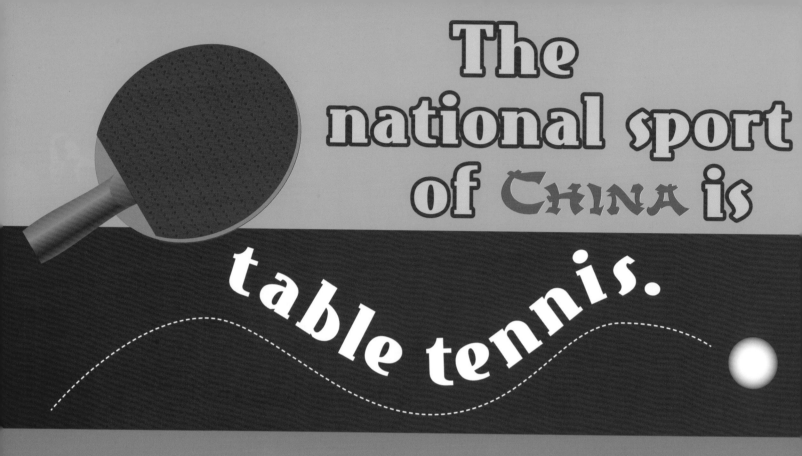

The national sport of China is table tennis.

SOFTBALL WAS INTRODUCED AS AN OLYMPIC SPORT FOR WOMEN IN THE 1996 SUMMER OLYMPICS. IN 2005, IT WAS REMOVED BY VOTE FROM THE 2012 AND 2016 SUMMER GAMES.

IN 1904, THE UNITED STATES HOSTED ITS FIRST OLYMPIC GAMES IN

ST. LOUIS, MISSOURI.

THE **DIMPLES** ON A GOLF BALL HELP IT

FLY THROUGH THE AIR FARTHER

THAN A BALL **WITHOUT DIMPLES.**

The **OLDEST** CONTINUOUS TROPHY in sports is the AMERICA'S CUP for YACHT RACING, which started in 1851.

USA 11

A2U

Stars & Stripes
619-255-4705

Drive to Hawaii
Kona Kai Resort
on Shelter Island – San Diego's Hawaiian Isle

Oversea
Yacht Insurance
(619) 222-1111

TEAMUSA11.COM

In 1975, Junko Tabei from Japan became the first woman to climb Mount Everest.

ROGER BANNISTER was the FIRST person to RUN a MILE in UNDER FOUR MINUTES. He did so in ENGLAND on May 6, 1954.

In 1457, golf was forbidden on Sundays in Scotland because it interfered with military training for wars against England.

During a **HOCKEY** game in 1959, a goalie was hit in the face by a puck so hard that he insisted on wearing a **MASK** he used only during practice for the rest of the game.

Now, ALL goalies wear MASKS.

FORBES FIELD, THE FIRST BASEBALL STADIUM IN THE UNITED STATES, WAS BUILT IN PITTSBURGH, PENNSYLVANIA, IN 1909.

The official state sport of South Dakota, Texas, and Wyoming is RODEO.

THE MAXIMUM LENGTH OF A

OF A

3 FEET

BASEBALL BAT IS

6 INCHES.

FISHING

is the

BIGGEST

participant **sport**

in the **WORLD.**

SOCCER FIELDS ARE CALLED

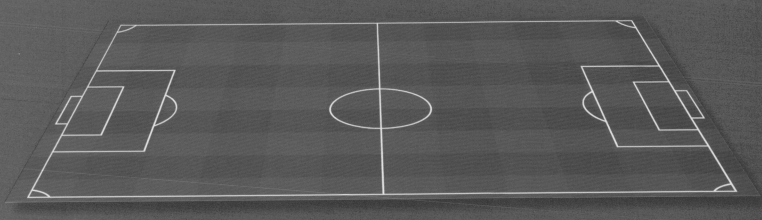

PITCHES.

THE ANCIENT GREEKS PRACTICED GYMNASTICS AS A WAY TO PREPARE FOR WAR, BECAUSE THE SPORT HELPED PRODUCE STRONG MUSCLES NECESSARY FOR HAND-TO-HAND COMBAT.

The **UnEvEn BaRs** is a **WOMEN'S** event in **GYMNASTICS** that started as the **MEN'S EVEN BARS** set to **DIFFERENT HEIGHTS.** The **D I S T A N C E** between the **TWO BARS** became **WIDER** as **TRICKS** became more **DIFFICULT.**

SUMO WRESTLING IS THE NATIONAL SPORT OF JAPAN

CANADA HAS WON 9 GOLD MEDALS IN OLYMPIC MEN'S ICE HOCKEY, MORE THAN ANY OTHER COUNTRY.

The first WORLD SERIES was in 1903 between PITTSBURGH and BOSTON and was a NINE-GAME contest. Boston WON the series 5-3.

The official state sport of MARYLAND is

JOUSTING.

The NEW YORK YANKEES have 27 WORLD SERIES titles, MORE than ANY OTHER team.

The word "checkmate" in CHESS comes from the PERSIAN expression *SHAH MAT,* which means "THE KING IS DEAD."

A BASKETBALL HOOP

NO DUNKING

is kept at a HEIGHT of 10 FEET.

THE TOUR DE FRANCE

is considered the **BIGGEST** TEST of **ENDURANCE** in **ALL** SPORTS.

OCTOPUSH, which is UNDERWATER HOCKEY, is popular in SOUTH AFRICA.

JAMES NAISMITH INVENTED BASKETBALL IN 1891 AND WROTE THE ORIGINAL RULEBOOK.

In American **FOOTBALL**, all players must wear a **NUMBER** between 1 and 99. Numbers 0 and 00 were once used in the **NFL**, but now they are only seen in **CANADIAN** football.

The **OLYMPICS** were **NOT** held in 1916, 1940, and 1944 due to

WORLD WAR I and **WORLD WAR II.**

Before it was a profession, a baseball umpire was an honorary position. Sometimes he would even sit in a

PADDED

ROCKING CHAIR

to view the game.

AFRICA, EUROPE, AND ASIA ALL HOLD THEIR OWN UNIQUE OLYMPIC GAMES. NORTH AND SOUTH AMERICA COMBINE TO MAKE THEIR OWN, TOO. IT'S CALLED THE PAN AMERICAN (OR PAN AM) GAMES.

TAE KWON DO means "way of the HAND and FOOT."

Hockey sticks were

STRAIGHT

until the 1960s, when a
Chicago Blackhawks
player introduced the

CURVE.

On a baseball diamond, the bases are **90** feet apart.

A softball infield is smaller.

On a softball diamond, the bases are **60** feet apart.

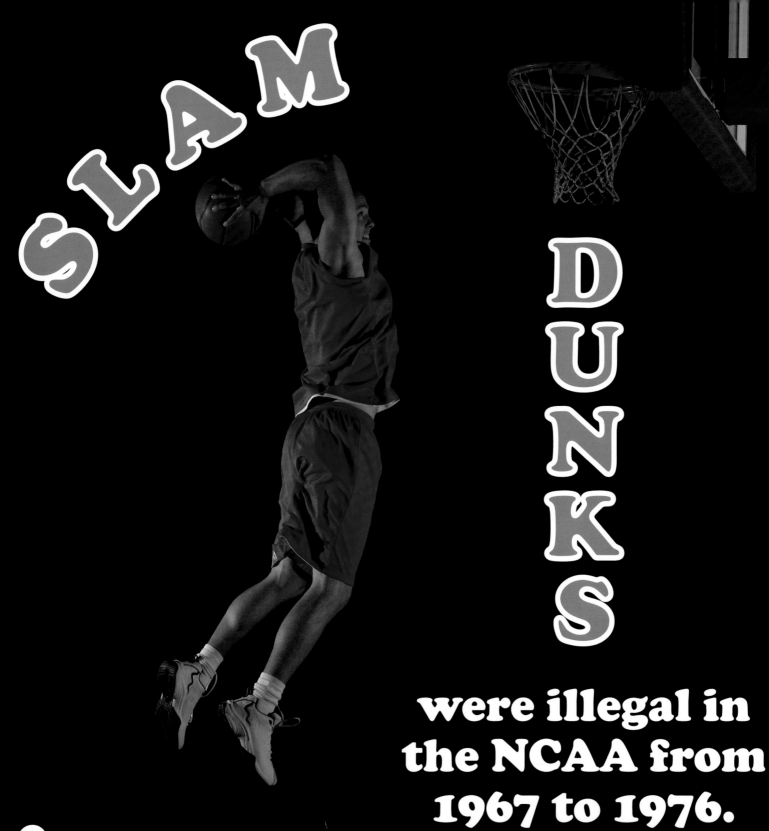

SLAM DUNKS

were illegal in the NCAA from 1967 to 1976.

The Australian Open, French Open, Wimbledon, and U.S. Open tennis tournaments make up the

GRAND SLAM.

THE GAME OF *Quidditch* FROM THE *Harry Potter* BOOK SERIES WAS ADAPTED INTO AN OFFICIAL COLLEGIATE SPORT IN THE UNITED STATES IN 2005.

Seven NFL TEAMS do NOT have CHEERLEADERS:

Buffalo BILLS

Chicago BEARS

Cleveland BROWNS

Detroit LIONS

Green Bay PACKERS

New York GIANTS

Pittsburgh STEELERS

ORIGINALLY, ICE SKATES WERE MERELY SHARPENED, FLATTENED ANIMAL BONES STRAPPED TO THE BOTTOM OF THE FEET.

THERE ARE ABOUT 11 MILLION ACTIVE SKATEBOARDERS IN THE WORLD.

Only goalies can touch the soccer ball with their hands.

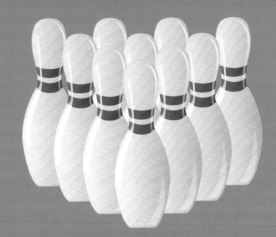

A **PERFECT** score in **BOWLING** is **300** points.

MANON RHEAUME WAS THE **FIRST WOMAN** TO PLAY IN A PRESEASON **EXHIBITION GAME** IN THE **NHL** AS THE **GOALIE** FOR THE **TAMPA BAY LIGHTNING.**

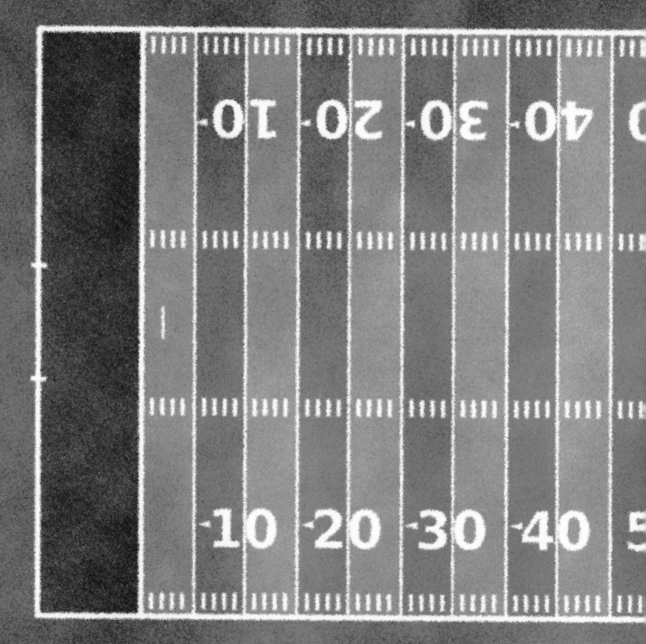

-10 -20 -30

-10 -20 -30 -40 5

120

A FOOTBALL FIELD IS

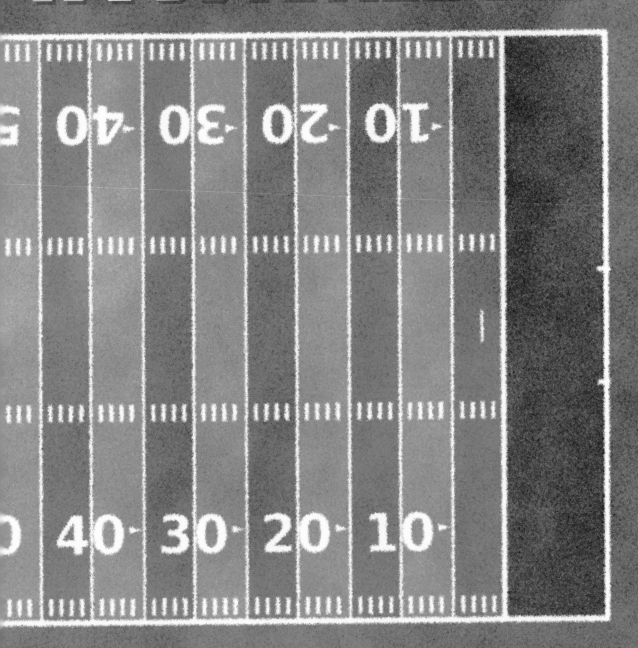

YARDS.

THE WORD "SOCCER" IS A BRITISH TERM THAT ORIGINATED IN ENGLAND IN THE LATE 1800S. SINCE 1980, USAGE OF THE WORD DECLINED IN ENGLAND.

BINGO

11	25	47	66	74
4	19	28	61	85
29	30	FREE ★ FREE	43	51
83	2	17	20	67
80	13	26	44	90

ON A BINGO CARD OF 90 NUMBERS, THERE ARE APPROXIMATELY **44 MILLION** WAYS TO MAKE A **B-I-N-G-O**

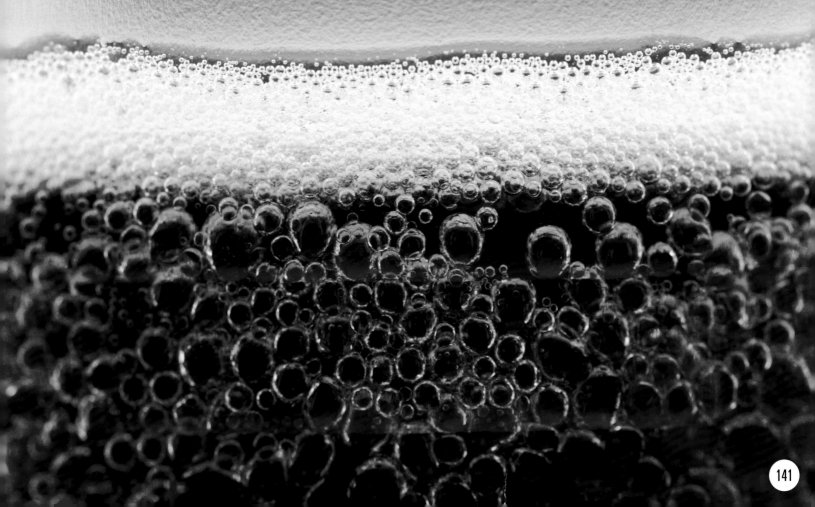

9,000 GALLONS of **PEPSI** products are sold at one **NASCAR** race weekend, enough to fuel **507** pit stops.

JEANNE GENEVIEVE GARNERIN was the first FEMALE PARACHUTIST. She JUMPED from a HOT AIR BALLOON in 1799.

THE 1912 SUMMER OLYMPICS IN STOCKHOLM, SWEDEN, WERE THE LAST GAMES IN WHICH GOLD MEDALS WERE ACTUALLY MADE OF SOLID GOLD.

In basketball, **UNSPORTSMANLIKE BEHAVIOR** by a player or coach is the most common technical violation, or **FOUL.**

The SLOWEST

swimming stroke is typically the

BREASTSTROKE.

THE NATIONAL SPORT OF NORWAY IS CROSS-COUNTRY SKIING.

IN THE ORIGINAL OFFICIAL BASEBALL RULES WRITTEN IN 1845, THE FIRST TEAM TO SCORE 21 RUNS WON THE GAME. THIS WAS REPLACED BY THE 9-INNING FORMAT IN 1857.

Because of a FOOTBALL'S resemblance to an OLIVE, the CHINESE often call the AMERICAN GAME of football "OLIVE BALL."

In order to allow PITCHERS to get a better GRIP, BASEBALLS are wiped down with 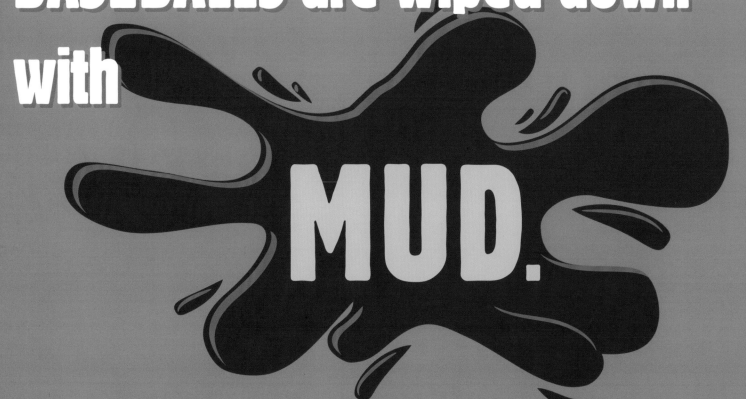 MUD.

A SOCCER BALL

is made up of **32** LEATHER PANELS

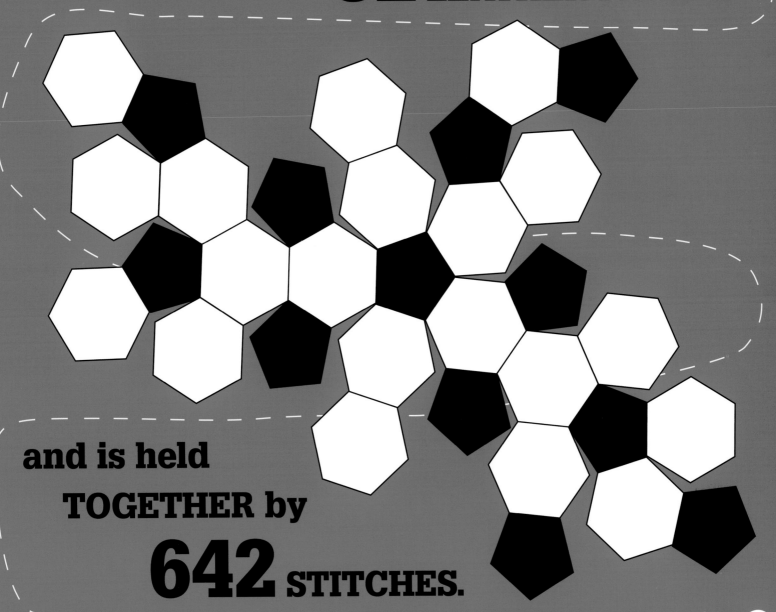

and is held TOGETHER by **642** STITCHES.

By Olympic rules, the

BADMINTON

BIRDIE

has to have exactly

16

FEATHERS.

THE FIRST BASKETBALL GAMES WERE PLAYED WITH **SOCCER** BALLS.

The most popular sports in FRANCE are soccer, tennis, and cycling.

A PERFECT GAME in **BASEBALL** is when the **SAME** player **PITCHES** the **ENTIRE** game **WITHOUT** allowing a player from the **OPPOSING** team to reach **BASE.**

Ninjutsu

is the

Japanese
art
of the
Ninja.

When ICE-SKATING was a new pastime in Europe, only members of the UPPER CLASS could participate.

In 1969, tensions between EL SALVADOR and HONDURAS were so highly charged that a few WORLD CUP matches between the two countries led to a THREE-DAY WAR.

In one SOCCER game, it is COMMON for a PLAYER to RUN about 6 MILES. This is EQUAL to running BACK and FORTH on a BASKETBALL court 350 TIMES.

Before automated pinsetters were invented in 1936, people used to manually reset bowling pins to the correct position, clear fallen pins, and return bowling balls to players.

It takes about
12,000 to 15,000 gallons
of water to make the ice
for a hockey rink.

THE PAR 77 INTERNATIONAL GOLF COURSE IN MASSACHUSETTS IS THE LONGEST COURSE IN THE WORLD AT 8,325 YARDS. THIS GOLF COURSE ALSO HAS THE LARGEST GREEN IN THE WORLD.

THE ORIGINS OF FIELD HOCKEY TRACE TO ANCIENT EGYPT AND PERSIA, MAKING IT ONE OF THE WORLD'S OLDEST KNOWN SPORTS.

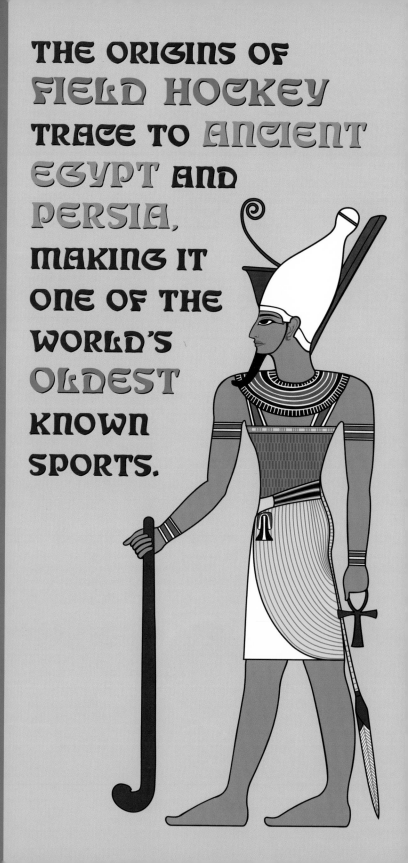

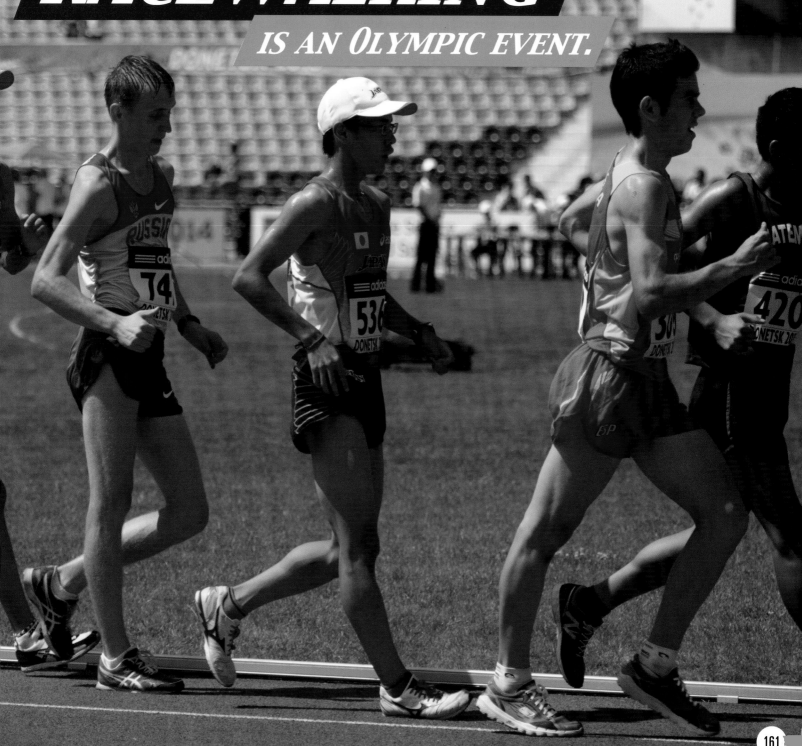

In horse racing, winning "HANDS DOWN" means the jockey NEVER raised his whip.

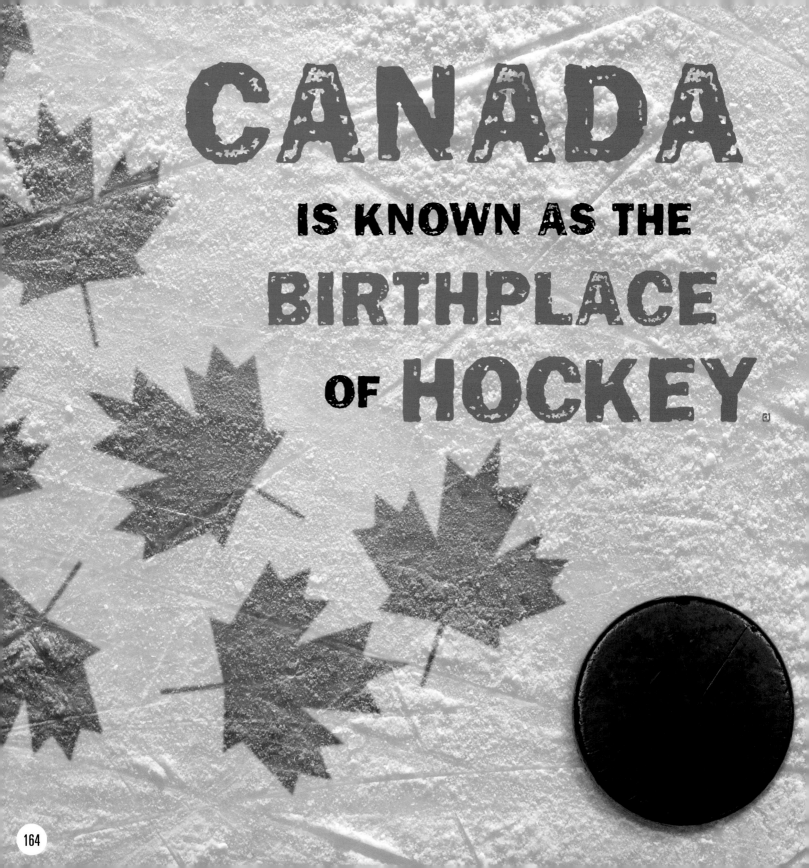

CANADA

IS KNOWN AS THE

BIRTHPLACE OF HOCKEY

The 2002 WORLD CUP was held in TWO places: SEOUL, South Korea, and TOKYO, Japan.

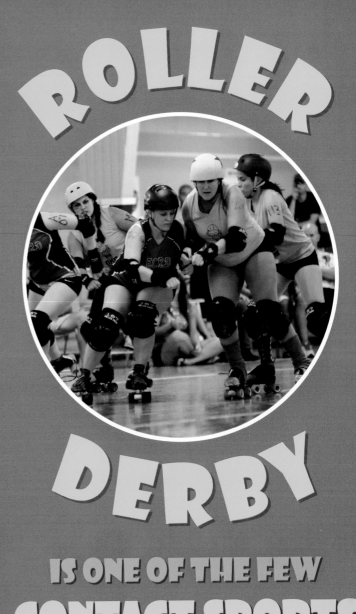

ROLLER DERBY IS ONE OF THE FEW CONTACT SPORTS DOMINATED BY FEMALE ATHLETES.

Baseballs are pitched OVERHAND, but

Softballs are pitched UNDERHAND.

The starting systems used in professional drag races are called

CHRISTMAS TREES.

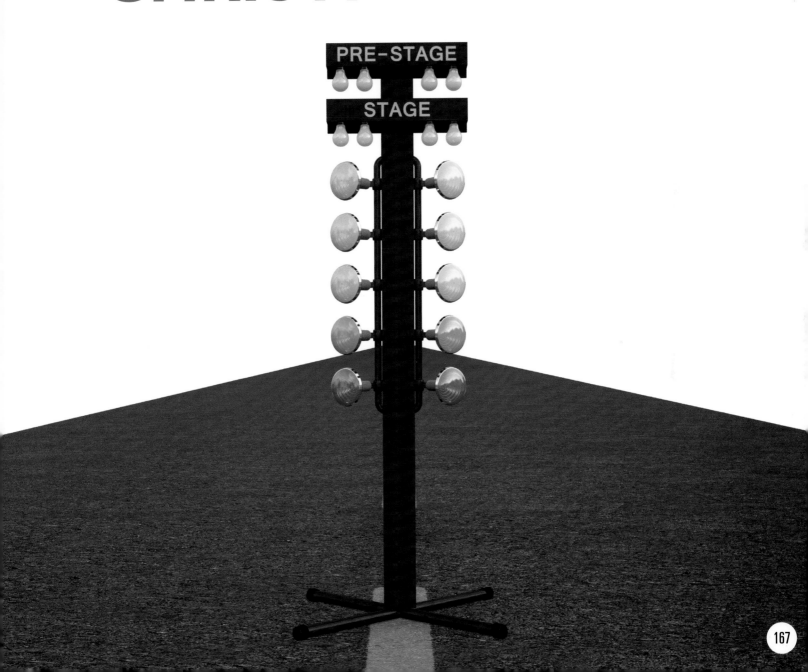

Golf balls can reach speeds of 170 miles per hour.

IF A GYMNAST IN THE OLYMPICS IS FOUND TO BE YOUNGER THAN 16, SHE AND HER TEAMMATES COULD BE STRIPPED OF THEIR MEDALS.

PARKOUR is a non-combative **MARTIAL ART** that emphasizes

FREE-FLOWING MOVEMENT
AROUND, OVER, and THROUGH

any environment.

It is also known as **FREE RUNNING,** and was based on military training obstacle courses.

THE TOUR DE FRANCE

CYCLING RACE WAS CREATED IN 1903 BY THE FRENCH NEWSPAPER L'AUTO TO HELP BOOST READERSHIP.

NATIVE AMERICANS played LACROSSE not just for FUN, but also to TRAIN WARRIORS for BATTLE and SETTLE ARGUMENTS between TRIBES.

The longest surf ride on a single natural wave was 37 minutes.

171

IN 1984, UWE HOHN OF GERMANY BECAME THE ONLY PERSON TO

THROW A JAVELIN

MORE THAN 100 METERS.

A NEW JAVELIN WAS DESIGNED TWO YEARS LATER ALONG WITH NEW RULES, MAKING HOHN'S ACCOMPLISHMENT AN "ETERNAL WORLD RECORD."

CRICKET

is the **SECOND MOST POPULAR SPORT** in the **WORLD.**

THE **LARGEST** ACTIVE SPORTS STADIUM IN THE WORLD WAS ONCE STRAHOV STADIUM IN **PRAGUE**, CZECH REPUBLIC, HOLDING UP TO **220,000** SPECTATORS. IT STOPPED HOLDING **ATHLETIC** EVENTS IN **1990.**

WOMEN WHO PLAYED IN THE FIRST WIMBLEDON TOURNAMENTS HAD TO WEAR FULL-LENGTH DRESSES.

CHESS

is a recognized sport of the International Olympic Committee.

BADMINTON was introduced in the United States in the late 19th century and became a popular sport in the 1930s.

The **RECORD** for the

D E E P E S T   F R E E   D I V E

(a **DIVE** into the ocean **WITHOUT** breathing equipment) **was set** in 2007 **by Herbert Nitsch of Austria.** He held his **BREATH for** more than **4 MINUTES, and** dove **214 METERS—** more than **the LENGTH of** 2 football fields.

Mary, Queen of Scots, was the **FIRST WOMAN** to play GOLF, in 1567.

In 2022, **BEIJING, CHINA,** will become the **ONLY** city to have hosted **BOTH** the **SUMMER** and **WINTER** Games since the beginning of the **MODERN OLYMPICS.**

The
average
HEIGHT
of an
OLYMPIC
medal-
winning
female
GYMNAST
is

5'1".

STARTING IN THE 1920s, OUTDOOR MINIATURE GOLF COURSES WERE BUILT ON ROOFTOPS IN NEW YORK CITY.

On a ROWING TEAM, the

MIDDLE  SEATS

are usually reserved for the

STRONGEST and

LARGEST rowers

to improve
the boat's BALANCE.

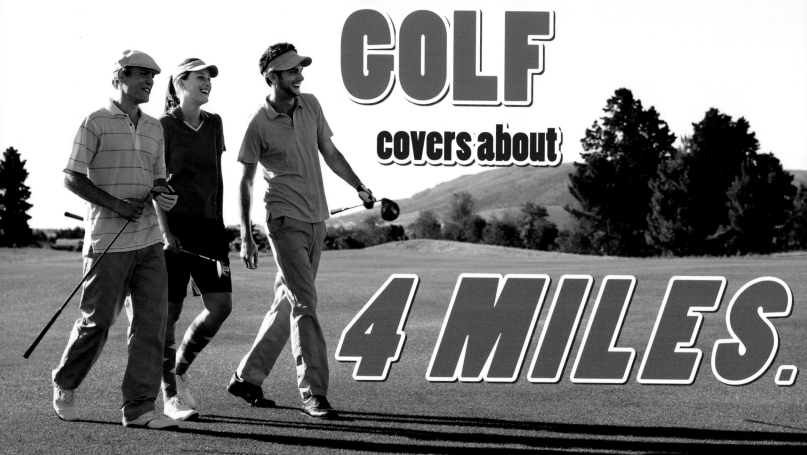

WALKING
18 holes of GOLF covers about 4 MILES.

ONLY GREECE HAS PARTICIPATED IN EVERY MODERN OLYMPIC GAMES.

The **NEW YORK METS** **were** cofounded **in 1962 by** **JOAN WHITNEY PAYSON,** **the** first **WOMAN** **to OWN an MLB team** **WITHOUT** inheriting **it.**

EVEN THOUGH LEFT-HANDED PEOPLE MAKE UP ONLY ABOUT 10% OF THE POPULATION, ABOUT 25% OF MAJOR LEAGUE BASEBALL PLAYERS ARE LEFTIES.

The sport of BOXING was introduced in 688 BC in GREECE, in the early stages of the ANCIENT Olympic Games.

COMPARED TO ROAD CAR
ENGINES THAT OPERATE
AT LESS THAN 7,000 RPM,
FORMULA ONE CAR ENGINES
OPERATE AT UP TO

15,000
RPM.

The **NATIONAL** sport of **INDIA**

is **FIELD HOCKEY.**

The popular sports drink GATORADE was named after the GATORS of the UNIVERSITY of FLORIDA, where it was developed in 1965.

KARATE is the MOST POPULAR MARTIAL ART

THE **LONGEST GAME** IN THE HISTORY OF PROFESSIONAL **BASEBALL** WAS PLAYED BY THE **ROCHESTER RED WINGS** AND THE **PAWTUCKET RED SOX** IN 1981. **THE GAME** LASTED **33 INNINGS,** WITH **11 HOURS** AND **25 MINUTES** OF **PLAYING** TIME.

TENNIS was one of the **FIRST** Olympic sports to have a **SEPARATE** competition for **WOMEN.**

The **ODDS** of making a

HOLE IN ONE

TWICE

in **ONE** round of **GOLF** are

67 million to 1.

MANY **TENNIS** PLAYERS BELIEVE IT IS **BAD LUCK** TO HOLD MORE THAN **TWO** BALLS AT A TIME WHEN **SERVING.**

YOU CANNOT PLAY POLO LEFT-HANDED.

The baseball
HOME PLATE is

inches wide.

The
national
sport of
SOUTH
KOREA
is
TAE
KWON DO.

THE **ZAMBONI**
WAS INVENTED IN 1949
BY FRANK ZAMBONI
TO KEEP **ICE RINKS**
PROPERLY MAINTAINED.

LOUIS X of FRANCE was the first person to make INDOOR TENNIS COURTS in the MODERN style.

RUGBY BALLS USED TO BE MADE OF PIG BLADDERS.

SOFTBALL is played on every CONTINENT in the WORLD except ANTARCTICA.

Many people think **ABNER DOUBLEDAY** invented baseball in 1839, but there is little evidence to prove this is true.

AMERICANS EAT ABOUT

1.25 BILLION

CHICKEN WINGS

OVER

SUPER BOWL

WEEKEND.

The word ARCHERY

is derived from the word

ARCUS,

a Latin term that means ARCH,

which a bow resembles.

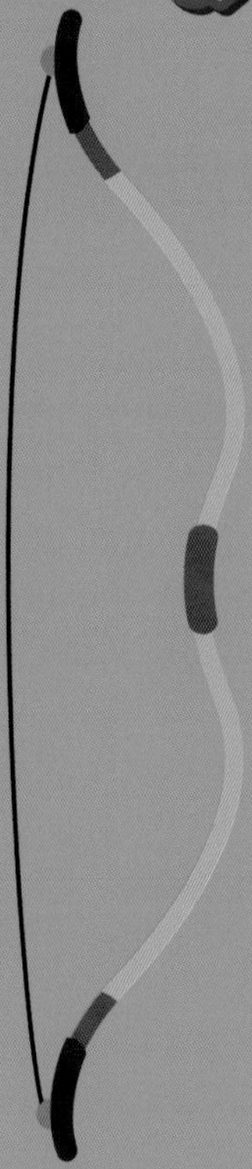

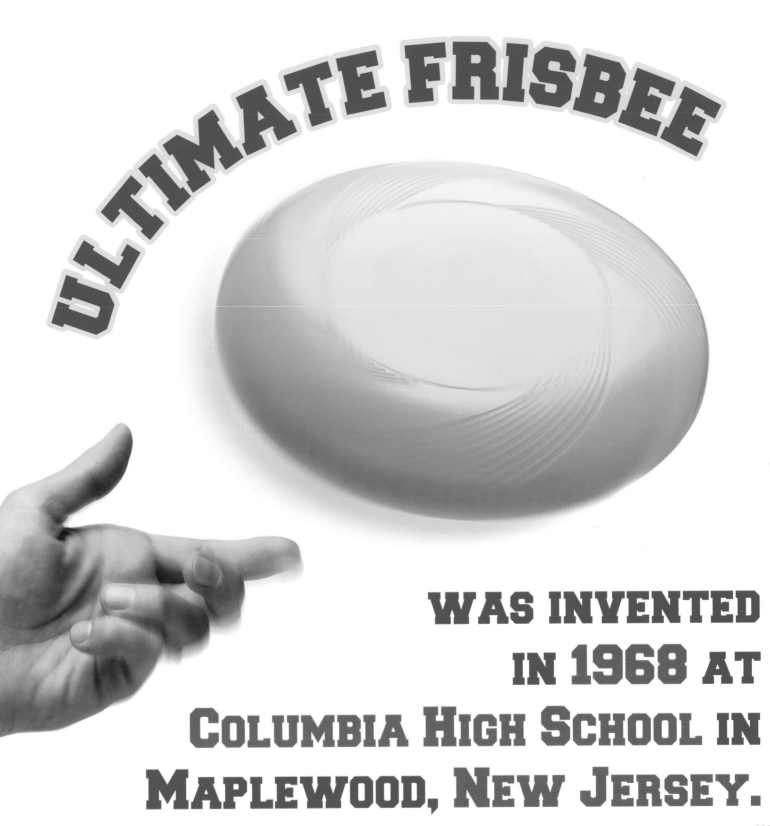

ULTIMATE FRISBEE WAS INVENTED IN 1968 AT COLUMBIA HIGH SCHOOL IN MAPLEWOOD, NEW JERSEY.

MLB teams use about 850,000 balls per season.

OCTOPUS WRESTLING

was a POPULAR SPORT on the WEST COAST of the United States in the 1960s.

The average LIFESPAN of an NBA basketball is

10,000 bounces.

The world record for LIMBO is

under 6 inches.

VOLLEYBALL IS THE SECOND MOST PLAYED SPORT IN THE WORLD.

DESPITE THE NAME, A SOFTBALL IS NOT VERY SOFT.

BRAZIL HAS WON 5 WORLD CUPS,

THE MOST SINCE THE TOURNAMENT BEGAN IN 1930.

A FACE-OFF IN HOCKEY WAS ORIGINALLY CALLED A

"PUCK-OFF."

SNOWBOARDING,

INVENTED IN 1965 IN THE UNITED STATES, WAS ORIGINALLY CALLED

"SNURFING"

BECAUSE RIDERS COULD

S U R F

ON SNOW.

BADMINTON
is the _FASTEST_
racquet sport
in the world, with
shuttlecock speeds
reaching more than
200 miles

per hour.

FENCING

was a popular form of STAGED ENTERTAINMENT *in 16th and 17th century* ENGLAND.

Before TEES were invented, GOLFERS used to play off HANDMADE SAND PILES.

The first FIFA WORLD CUP in AFRICA was hosted in 2010 by SOUTH AFRICA.

GOLF BALLS TRAVEL FARTHER IN HOT TEMPERATURES THAN IN COLD

THE LO

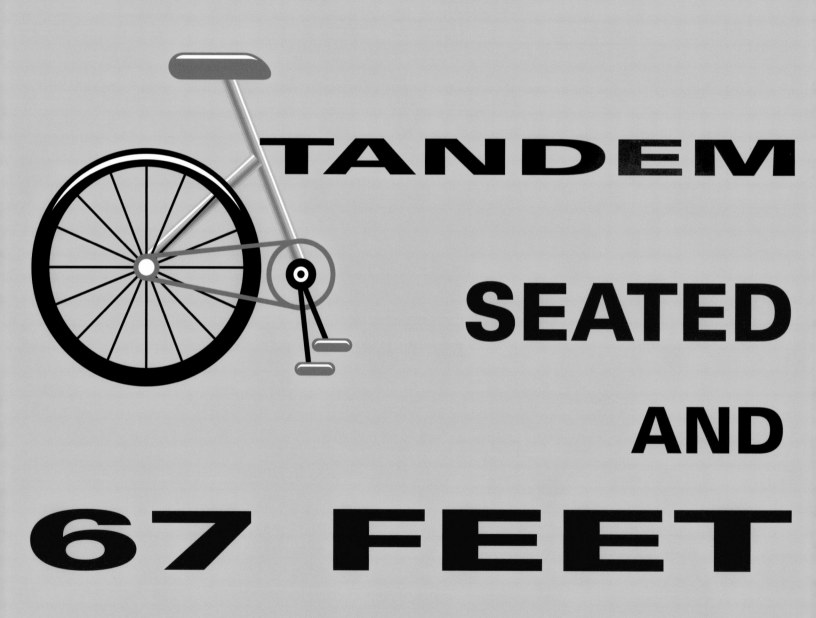

TANDEM

SEATED

AND

67 FEET

NGEST

BICYCLE

35 PEOPLE

WAS

LONG.

THE SEATTLE MARINERS BASEBALL TEAM IS OWNED BY THE VIDEO GAME COMPANY NINTENDO.

HONEY

was used as the center of **GOLF BALLS** until the 1960s, when a synthetic liquid with similar properties was invented.

THERE ARE **366** DIMPLES ON A GOLF BALL.

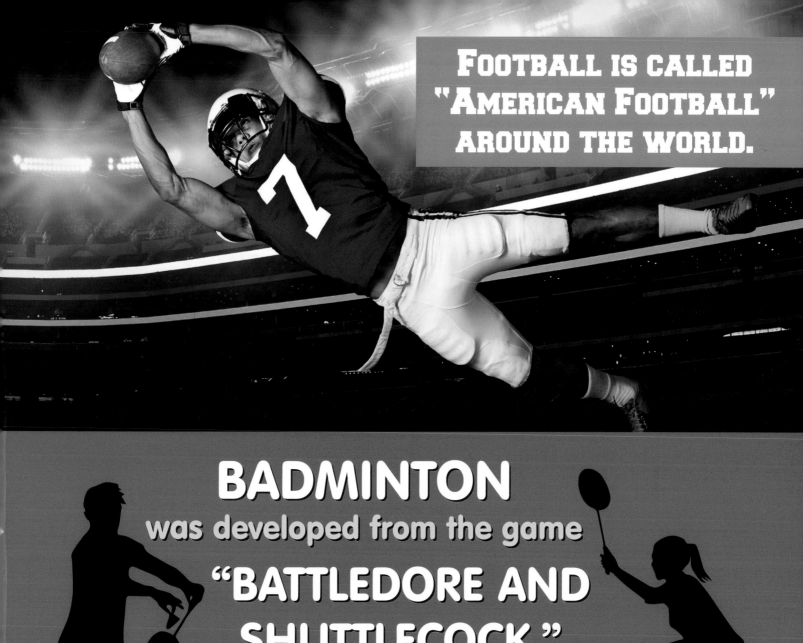

FOOTBALL IS CALLED "AMERICAN FOOTBALL" AROUND THE WORLD.

BADMINTON

was developed from the game

"BATTLEDORE AND SHUTTLECOCK."

Two people with small rackets called battledores would hit a shuttlecock back and forth, except **WITHOUT A NET** in between.

HORSE RACING

IN THE UNITED STATES DATES BACK TO 1665, WHEN THE FIRST RACETRACK WAS CONSTRUCTED ON LONG ISLAND, NEW YORK.

SOME FORM OF BOWLING IS PLAYED IN MORE THAN 90 COUNTRIES AROUND THE WORLD.

It is a common SUPERSTITION that GOLF BALLS with a number HIGHER THAN 4 are BAD LUCK.

THERE ARE MORE THAN ONE BILLION BICYCLES IN THE WORLD.

The ORIGINAL NAME for ICE HOCKEY was HURLEY.

During the 1900s, LACROSSE

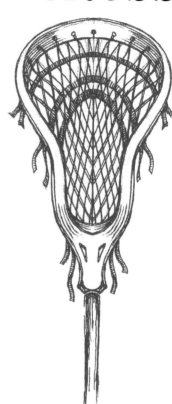

was primarily a regional sport in the United States centered around the East Coast.

THE ONLY NUMBER TO BE RETIRED UNIVERSALLY BY MLB IS 42 FOR JACKIE ROBINSON.

FALLING off of a surfboard or **COLLIDING** with others is called a **WIPEOUT.**

Only two NFL teams have MARCHING BANDS: The Baltimore RAVENS and the Washington REDSKINS.

There are
more than
30

women's WORLD CUP SKIING events that take place WORLDWIDE.

The first skateboards were made with wooden boxes or boards, with roller skate wheels attached to the bottom.

The first major stadium to use **artificial grass** was the Astrodome in Houston, Texas, which led to the nickname

"AstroTurf."

THE MLB PITCHER WITH THE MOST CAREER STRIKEOUTS IS NOLAN RYAN WITH 5,714.

THE **WORLD CUP** IS THE **BIGGEST SOCCER TOURNAMENT** IN THE **WORLD** AND IS HELD EVERY **FOUR YEARS** IN A **DIFFERENT COUNTRY**.

IN ANCIENT GREECE, MOST GYMNASTIC COMPETITIONS WERE DONE IN THE NUDE. "GYMNASTICS" COMES FROM THE GREEK WORD *GYMNOS*, WHICH MEANS "NAKED."

SPITTING INTO YOUR HAND BEFORE PICKING UP A BASEBALL BAT IS SAID TO BRING GOOD LUCK.

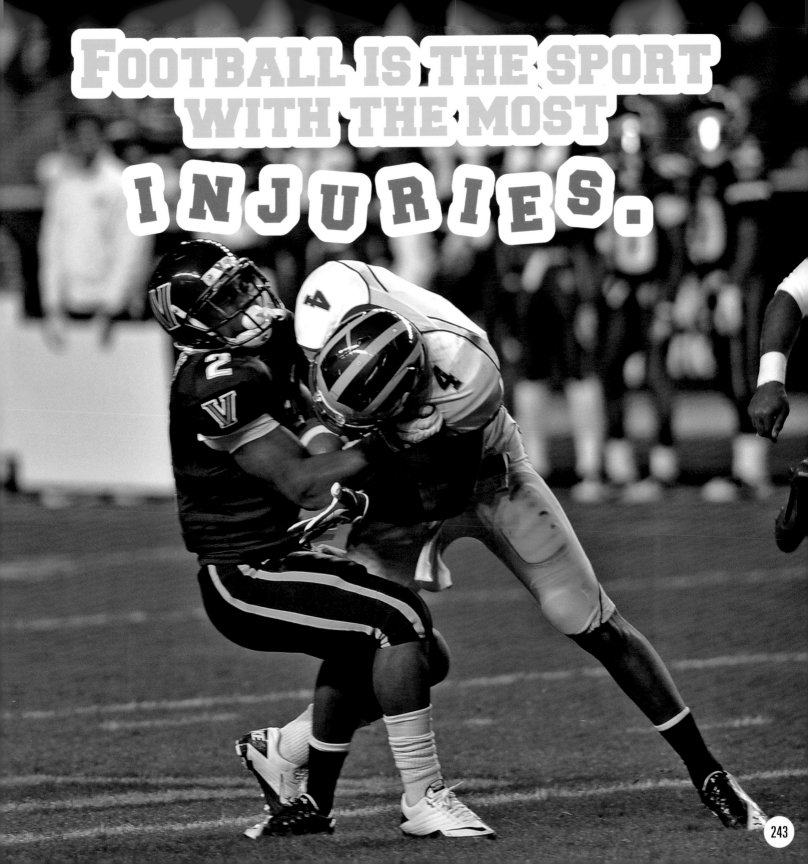

FOOTBALL IS THE SPORT WITH THE MOST INJURIES.

SEPAK TAKRAW, or kick ball, is a type of **VOLLEYBALL** played in southeastern **ASIA** where players are **NOT** allowed to use their **HANDS.**

The first **NFL** team to put its **logo** on its helmets was the **Los Angeles Rams** in 1948.

The national sports of CANADA are

LACROSSE
in the summer

&

HOCKEY
in the winter.

The
BLACK BELT
in martial arts
doesn't always
represent the
**HIGHEST SKILL
LEVEL.**

In many
disciplines, it is
merely a symbol of
**UNDERSTANDING
THE BASICS.**

NADIA COMANECI

of Romania was the first **GYMNAST** to score a

PERFECT

10

at the **OLYMPIC GAMES** in 1976 in **MONTREAL**.

(A perfect 10 is no longer possible due to scoring changes.)

NORWAY
HAS WON
329
MEDALS
AT THE
WINTER
OLYMPIC
GAMES,
MORE THAN
ANY OTHER
COUNTRY.

Mongolian and Sumo

WREsTLING

only allow the **FEET** to

TOUCH THE GROUND.

In Pesäpallo, or **FINNISH BASEBALL**, the bases are set in a near zIG-zAG pattern and the ball is thrown **UPWARD** instead of *FORWARD*.

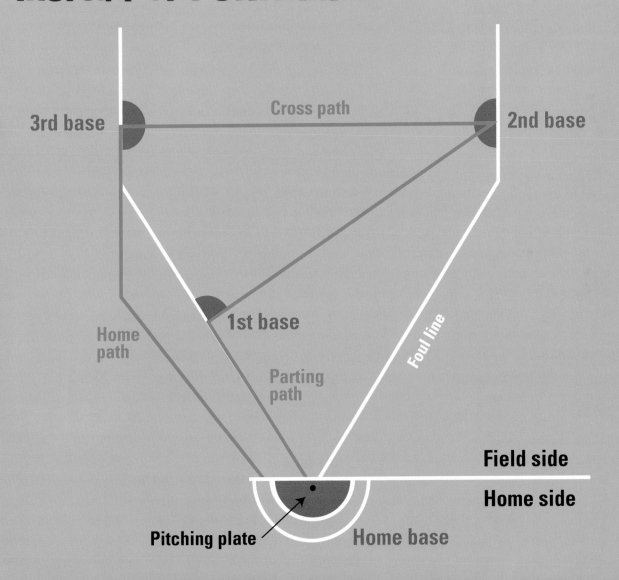

3rd base

Cross path

2nd base

Home path

1st base

Parting path

Foul line

Field side

Home side

Pitching plate

Home base

Competitive

KARUTA

is a Japanese sport that involves MATCHING spoken classical poems to their WRITTEN CARDS. Each match lasts about 90 MINUTES, with 5 to 7 matches per tournament. Karuta tournaments are known for being so INTENSE, some players LOSE up to 4 POUNDS by the end.

紫　式　部

巡りあひて
見しや夫とも
わかぬまに
雲がくれにし
夜半の月かな